For Imogen, Morwenna and Finn
M.M.

For Emily and Alex
L.C.

First published in 2001 in Great Britain by
Gullane Children's Books

Text © Miriam Moss 2001
Illustrations © Lynne Chapman 2001

This 2008 edition published by Sandy Creek
by arrangement with Gullane Children's Books
185 Fleet Street, London, EC4A 2HS, United Kingdom

Sandy Creek, 122 Fifth Avenue, New York, NY 10011

ISBN-13: 978-1-4351-0922-3

10 9 8 7 6 5 4 3 2 1

Printed and bound in Indonesia

A New House

Miriam Moss
Illustrated by Lynne Chapman

SANDY CREEK

Plop! Plop! Plop! went the rainwater into the bucket.
"This is no good," said Stripe. "I think we'll have
to move."
Smudge stared at him. "I'm not moving," she said.

"But this house is too small," said Stripe, "and the roof keeps leaking."
"This is my home," said Smudge, "and there's nothing wrong with it. And even if there is," she added, "I like it."

"I've seen a lovely new house," said Stripe later.
"We could go and look at it if you like."
Smudge just sipped her drink.

"Smudge," said Stripe after a while, "remember your favorite old pants? You grew out of them, didn't you? Well, did you know you can grow out of your house too?" "People don't wear houses," said Smudge. "Anyway, this house still fits me."

"Wouldn't it be nice to have a garden?"
said Stripe, as Smudge watered a snail.
"We might find a new house," continued Stripe,
"that has a little river running through the garden."

"Do you mean a real river? With little fish in it?
A river you can paddle in?" asked Smudge.

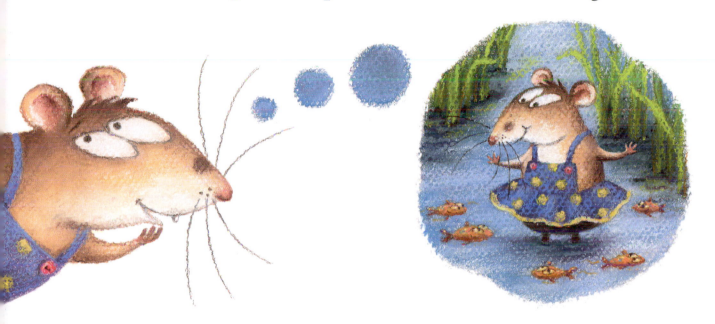

"Mmm," said Stripe. "We might even get a boat."
Smudge went to her room, to think.

"Oh, look!" said Stripe, as they walked through the woods that afternoon, "there's that house I was telling you about. The one that could be our new house."

"It doesn't look new to me," said Smudge. "It looks old."
"That's because no one has lived in it for years,"
said Stripe. "Come on, let's look inside!"

The front door creaked open. Great grey cobwebs hung everywhere. "Ugh!" cried Smudge. "I can't live here!"

But then Stripe showed her the garden. It was huge.
Smudge ran across the lawn and opened a little red gate.
"Look, Stripe!" she called excitedly,
"there's a real river, just like you said!"

The next day, they visited the house again.
Stripe took down the moldy old curtains,
while Smudge tried out the bath.

Then she slid down the banisters, discovered a trap door
in the kitchen and made a den under the stairs.

Smudge and Stripe had a wonderful time painting
the new house, room by room, until it looked
brand new. Smudge painted her room bright
yellow to match the daffodils in the garden.

When the day came to move from the old house, Stripe gave Smudge a special box to pack her things in. Smudge looked worried. "How do you know what to pack and what to leave behind?" she asked. "Well," said Stripe, "let's leave the walls, the floor and the roof." "You forgot the holes in the ceiling," Smudge laughed.

At last everything was packed.
And, when the last box was tied on,
they said goodbye to the empty house.

At the new house, Smudge had fun unloading,
unpacking and unwrapping all their things.
Suddenly she shouted: "I . . . can't . . .
find Perkins! Perkins is lost!"
"He won't be lost," said Stripe gently, "he's just
not unpacked yet."

Sure enough, they found Perkins packed
down the back of the piano. That night,
all three of them slept in the same room.

"Isn't this great," sighed Stripe the next day as they wandered down to the river. "Our first whole day in our new home! And look, here's a surprise for you!"

Tied to a post was a little red boat.
"Oh!" cried Smudge, "A boat!
Can we go in it right now?"
"What a good idea!" said Stripe.

Much later, while Stripe took a nap
by the fire, Smudge drew a picture.

She left her picture on the table for
Stripe to see. Then she went upstairs
to tuck Perkins into his new bed.